Real People

Sandra Day O'Connor

By Mary Hill

Welcome
Books™

Children's Press®
A Division of Scholastic Inc.
New York / Toronto / London / Auckland / Sydney
Mexico City / New Delhi / Hong Kong
Danbury, Connecticut

Photo Credits: Cover. p. 5 © Roger Ressmeyer/Corbis; pp. 7, 9, 11 © Bettmann/Corbis;
p. 13 © Steve Northup/TimePix; pp. 15, 19 © Corbis; pp. 17, 21 © AP/Wide World Photos
Contributing Editor: Jennifer Silate
Book Design: Daniel Hosek

Library of Congress Cataloging-in-Publication Data

Hill, Mary, 1977-
    Sandra Day O'Connor / by Mary Hill.
    p. cm. — (Real people)
    Includes bibliographic references and index.
    Summary: An easy-to-read biography of Sandra Day O'Connor who, in 1981,
    became the first woman appointed a Supreme Court justice.
    ISBN 0-516-25868-0 (lib. bdg.) — ISBN 0-516-27890-8 (pbk.)
    1. O'Connor, Sandra Day, 1930—-Juvenile literature. 2.
    Judges—United States—Biography—Juvenile literature. 3. United
    States. Supreme Court—Biography—Juvenile literature. [1. O'Connor,
    Sandra Day, 1930- 2. Judges. 3. United States. Supreme Court—Biography.
    4. Women—Biography.] I. Title. II. Series: Real people (Childrens Press)

    KF8745.O25 H55 2003
    347.73'2634—dc21

                                                    200215267

Contents

Meet Sandra Day O'Connor.

She is a very **famous** person.

Sandra Day O'Connor was born in 1930.

She lived in Texas.

7

Sandra went to **college**.

She studied to become a **lawyer**.

9

Sandra is **married** to John O'Connor.

They have three sons.

11

Sandra Day O'Connor became a **judge**.

She worked very hard.

13

In 1981, Sandra became a **Supreme Court justice**.

She was the first woman to have that job.

15

Sandra works with other Supreme Court justices.

They make important **decisions** for the United States.

Sandra works with many important people.

She has worked with presidents and other leaders.

19

Sandra Day O'Connor has a very important job.

She works hard for the United States.

21

New Words

college (**kol**-ij) a place of higher learning where students can continue to study after they have finished high school

decisions (di-**sizh**-uhns) making up one's mind about things

famous (**fay**-muhs) being known by many people

judge (**juhj**) a person who listens to cases before a court and decides how a guilty person should be punished

lawyer (**law**-yur) a person who is trained to explain the law to people and who acts and speaks for them in court

married (**mar**-eed) having a husband or wife

Supreme Court justice (suh-**preem kort juhss**-tiss) a judge for the highest and most powerful court in the United States

To Find Out More

Books

Meet My Grandmother: She's a Supreme Court Justice
by Courtney O'Connor
Millbrook Press

Sandra Day O'Connor
by Gini Holland
Raintree Publishers

Web Site
Oyez, Oyez, Oyez: Sandra Day O'Connor
http://oyez.org/justices/justices.cgi?justice_id=102
Learn about Sandra Day O'Connor's life and career on this Web site.

Index

About the Author
Mary Hill writes and edits children's books.

Reading Consultants
Kris Flynn, Coordinator, Small School District Literacy, The San Diego County
Office of Education

Shelly Forys, Certified Reading Recovery Specialist, W.J. Zahnow Elementary
School, Waterloo, IL

Sue McAdams, Former President of the North Texas Reading Council of the
IRA, and Early Literacy Consultant, Dallas, TX